What's Happening to Grandpa?

by Maria Shriver

Illustrated by Sandra Speidel

Little, Brown, and Company
and
Warner Books

Boston • New York

Little, Brown and Company and Warner Books

Time Warner Book Group
1271 Avenue of the Americas, New York, NY 10020
Visit our Web site at www.lb-kids.com

First Edition

ISBN 0-316-00101-5
LCCN 2003111975

10 9 8 7 6 5 4 3 2 1

PHX

Designed by Ellen Jacob and Pegi Goodman

Printed in the United States of America

The illustrations for this book were done in pastels on Bristol board.
The text was set in Calligraphic 810 BT, and the display type is Wade Sans Light.

Acknowledgments

So many of the same people have helped me with all three of my children's books–
What's Heaven?, What's Wrong with Timmy?, and now What's Happening
to Grandpa? I thank them all for their consistency, integrity, and insights.
What's Happening to Grandpa? would not have been possible without the patience,
wisdom, and invaluable assistance of Teri Hess. She helped me with every draft, and
I am deeply grateful as always for her loyalty, support, her wise suggestions, and her encouragement.
A big thanks to my wonderful, loyal, and tenacious agent, Jan Miller,
and her hardworking assistant, Shannon Miser-Marven. You make me shine, and
I'm so honored to work with you. I can't say enough about my talented creative director, Ellen Jacob,
whose skill with people is as sensitive as her skill with text and images.
Thank you also to my editor, Rick Horgan, for always understanding me and supporting me.
Andrea Spooner, thank you for your help and insights. To Camille McDuffie—You are an angel who
always makes sure that everyone knows about my work. All of you believed in the message of this
book from the start, and I am extremely grateful for your support.
My thanks also to Shari Lichtner, Alyssa Morris, and Christine Cuccio of Little, Brown,
and Pegi Goodman. Without your dedication this book wouldn't have been possible.
Finally, it continues to be an honor to work with Sandra Speidel,
the remarkably gifted illustrator of all three of my books for children. Her belief in
the message of this book is evident on every page.

Also by
Maria Shriver

What's Heaven?

What's Wrong with Timmy?

Ten Things I Wish I'd Known —
Before I Went Out into the Real World

Dedication

*For my amazing children, Katherine, Christina, Patrick, and Christopher,
and my remarkable husband, Arnold. Your love and laughter fulfill me every day,
and your existence gives meaning and purpose to my life.
To my brothers, Bobby, Timothy, Mark, and Anthony. Your encouragement, patience,
wisdom, and support made this book possible. Thank you from the bottom of my heart.
And to my parents, Eunice and Sargent Shriver. You have always been extraordinary
role models to me. Now more than ever I want you to know how much I admire
and love each of you. I marvel at the journey you embarked on more
than fifty years ago and the path you still walk together.*

XOXO
Maria

*For my father, Louis H. Speidel, Jr.
Every day I remember your generosity, kindness, and love.*

Sandy

Once upon a time there was a girl named Kate. She was curious, sensitive, and wise beyond her age. Her younger brothers and sister looked up to her and thought she knew the answers to everything. Kate's parents had taught her to celebrate life, be kind to friends, be respectful of teachers, and always, always to stick up for your *family.*

"Family" was a big deal in Kate's home. In fact, every Sunday Kate and her brothers and sister visited their grandparents. Kate felt lucky to have the grandparents she had. Her grandma was a lot of fun and very funny. She was the kind of grandma who enjoyed giving tea parties and playing games like Chinese checkers and croquet. In the summer, she loved to look for mermaids in the ocean or build sand castles for princesses, and when she went swimming, she always wore a bathing cap with big, bright flowers on it. When Kate took long walks with her, she talked about her "conversations with the angels." Kate thought her grandma was so cool.

As for Grandpa . . . well, he was a character. He didn't talk to angels—he talked to God. At least that's what he told Kate. He loved baseball, classical music, and eating potato chips — lots and lots of potato chips. Most of all, Grandpa loved to tell all kinds of stories and charmed everyone with his tales about baseball, his life on a submarine, and riding his bike through Europe. As her mom often told Kate, Grandpa was "one of a kind." To Kate, neither of her grandparents seemed old. In fact, she was sure they thought of themselves as kids. That's one of the reasons she loved being with them so much.

One Sunday, while visiting with her grandparents, Kate noticed that her grandpa was repeating the same stories. He kept asking the same questions over and over. And when she asked him about his day, he couldn't seem to remember what he'd just done. ❧ At first Kate didn't think much about it. She knew some older people had trouble reading, some couldn't hear like they once did, and some couldn't even walk very well anymore. So, forgetting a few things didn't seem like a big deal to her.

But one weekend while Kate was making lemonade in the kitchen, she heard her grandpa banging drawers in the hall and complaining that he couldn't find his keys. She watched as her grandma tried to tell Grandpa that he wasn't allowed to drive anymore and that she would drive him to the store. Grandpa threw down his books, yelled, and then turned and slammed the door. This behavior wasn't like Grandpa at all! Kate watched as her grandma stood alone in the hall, put her face in her hands, and began to cry. Kate's mother rushed in, wrapped her arms around Grandma, and held her just as tightly as she held Kate when she cried. Kate quietly turned away and went back to the kitchen to finish her lemonade.

After several more weekend visits with Grandpa, it was clear to Kate that something was wrong with him. She went to her mom and said, "Grandpa keeps repeating himself; he can't seem to remember what he just did. I saw him yell at Grandma, and then this morning he didn't remember my name. Mom," she said, "what's happening to Grandpa?" ☙ Tears welled up in her mom's eyes, and for a moment there was silence. Kate hated silence — it made her uncomfortable. Then in a quiet but strong voice Kate's mom said, "Sweetheart, Grandpa went to the doctor recently because he wanted to find out why he was having problems remembering so many things. Some memory loss is quite normal for older people, so we didn't know whether to be worried or not. The doctor decided to give Grandpa lots of tests to find out if his problem was something different. ☙ When the tests came back, the doctor found out your grandpa has a condition called Alzheimer's. It's a disease of the brain that some people get when they're older. It affects Grandpa's memory and makes him confused, irritated, and often angry because he's struggling to remember things he just did or conversations he just had. It's really hard for him, and it's devastating for Grandma and me to see someone we love and with whom we've shared our whole lives go off into his own world." ❧ Kate was stunned. Her grandpa had Alz's-something-or-other. What did that mean for him? For her grandma? For her mom? For their family? How would she explain this to her brothers and sister? Kate's mind raced. She had so many questions, so many feelings, so many fears. For a few minutes Kate just stared into space. Then she said in a quiet voice, "What do we do now? What's going to happen to Grandpa?"

Kate's mother took a deep breath and looked her right in the eye. "Honey, what we do now is support Grandma and just keep on loving and respecting Grandpa the way we always have. We're going to have to be more patient with him and more understanding. It's going to be hard, but it's important for you and your brothers and sister to understand that Grandpa doesn't mean to be annoying when he asks the same question over and over. It's just that his brain isn't working the same way that it used to, and so he struggles to remember things he just did. He still enjoys talking about experiences he had many years ago. But the time will come when he won't be able to recall memories from long ago, either."

Kate thought about that for a long time. If Grandpa had Alzheimer's, did that mean her mom was going to get it? Would Kate get it too? ❧

Sensing her daughter's anxiety, Kate's mom said, "Just because Grandpa has Alzheimer's doesn't mean I'm going to get it or that anyone else in our family will. Some people get it when they grow older, and many others don't. Some who have Alzheimer's continue to live at home, but others are better off living in a place where they can receive special care. We're also learning more every day about how doctors can help people like Grandpa. Someday there will be a cure." ❧ "But what about now?" asked Kate. "Is Grandpa going to change? Is he going to be a different kind of grandpa from now on?" Kate's mom reached out and stroked her daughter's hair. "There's no way to tell, honey. One day he probably won't know who we are. That's why it's so important to cherish who he is today."

Kate couldn't believe that one day her grandpa might not know who she is. It seemed impossible. She looked over at Grandpa, who was sitting on the porch reading his paper. She tried to imagine him as a little boy her age with his whole life in front of him. She thought about how handsome he looked in those "olden day" pictures around her home, and about his love of storytelling. Her favorite stories that Grandpa told were the ones about how he fell in love with Grandma. Now Kate wondered who would tell those stories to her sister and brothers. She asked herself, Is there something I can do to help Grandpa? Some way to make it easier for him? That night, when Kate went to bed, she was convinced that she would come up with an idea.

The next day, Kate was having lunch with her best friends in the school yard. As they excitedly discussed going to the movies on Sunday, Kate suddenly found herself thinking about Grandpa. She wanted to see him on Sunday more than anything. But would her friends understand? Did any of their grandparents have Alzheimer's or other problems remembering things? What did their grandparents think about getting old? Were they scared? Were they lonely? Were they sad or happy?

Kate knew that her friend Rachel's grandma was "wild" — at least that's how Rachel described her. She had a purple golf cart, a purple room, and a dog with purple bows. Rachel's grandpa was equally "out there." He did push-ups and drank protein drinks all day long, and he drove a sports car. Keesha's grandma was in heaven, and her grandpa lived with her family. Tina's grandma, Nana, loved to travel. She was always sending postcards from some faraway place. Roger's grandpa, whom Roger called Papa, baby-sat him all the time because both of his parents worked a lot. He collected trains and also taught Roger how to play chess and jacks. And then there was Julia. Kate felt sorry for her. She didn't have any grandparents at all. Kate couldn't imagine her life without her grandparents.

As her friends gabbed about their weekend plans, Kate's mind was far, far away. She thought about her mom and how she must feel about what was happening to Grandpa. Her mom admired her father so much. She had always told Kate that Grandpa was the smartest man in the world. He had taught her how to play baseball and tennis just like her brothers. He'd taken her on trips and shown her different cultures and religions. He was hardworking, kind, charming, funny, considerate of others, and, just like Kate, curious about everything.

Wow! It must be hard, Kate thought, for her mom to watch Grandpa grow old. Kate hated the idea of her own parents getting old. She wanted them to stay young forever. ☙ But she knew they couldn't. At that moment Kate knew that she needed to be with Grandpa and her family this weekend and not with her friends. She needed to explain to them why she couldn't be with them on Sunday. She wanted them to understand what was happening to her grandpa so that if they met him, they wouldn't laugh at him or think his behavior was strange. ☙ "You guys," said Kate, taking a deep breath, "I have something to tell you." Everyone looked over at Kate. "I just found out my grandpa has Alzheimer's." Suddenly, everyone was quiet. ☙ "All-what?" asked Tina. ☙ "Alzheimer's," said Roger. ☙ "What's that?" said Rachel, twirling a strand of hair around her finger. "Is it contagious, or is it like cancer?" ◎ "No," said Kate. "Alzheimer's is when you lose your memory. You get confused and ask the same things over and over. It starts slow and gets worse with time." ◎ "That must be really awful, not being able to remember people and stuff," said Keesha. "Now that I think about it, it must be really hard to get old. You lose your friends, you don't always feel so great, and people probably don't invite you out a lot." ◎ "Yeah," said Kate, "that's why my mom tries to include my grandparents in everything we do. She says it's important to share as much as I can with them and to ask lots of questions about their lives so I can learn from their experiences." ◎ All of a sudden Kate got a great idea. She was sure Grandpa would love it. She couldn't wait to visit him next Sunday!

On Sunday morning when Grandpa opened the door, a huge smile spread across his face. He hugged everyone and roared with laughter as Kate's little brother showed him his new Irish jig. While her siblings played football at the far end of the lawn and her mom strolled with Grandma down the path to the garden, Kate sat on the porch with her grandpa. He brought her a glass of her favorite lemonade and a big bowl of his favorite chips.

"Grandpa," said Kate, "would it be okay if the two of us made a scrapbook of your life? I brought some of your olden-day photos and some pictures of me and my family too. You can tell me the story behind each picture, and then together we'll put them in the album." ☙ Grandpa laughed. "That's a fantastic idea," he said, peering eagerly into the box she'd brought. Kate started by showing Grandpa an old picture of him as a little boy. He held it tightly and for a minute said nothing; then he began talking. "When I was a kid I loved to play baseball. That's a photo of me using my fastball to toss a no-hitter."

For a moment he seemed lost in thought, as if he were reliving that long-ago game. "In fact," Grandpa said, "I taught your mother how to pitch that fastball. Did she ever tell you that?" ❧ Kate nodded, wondering what his childhood was like when he wasn't playing baseball. "Grandpa," she said, "were you happy when you were a little boy?" ❧ "Absolutely," said Grandpa with a smile. ❧ "Can you remember a lot from those times?" asked Kate. ❧ "The truth is, honey, I'm having trouble remembering many things lately," said Grandpa. "In fact, a few months ago the doctors told me I have early stages of something called Alzheimer's. To be honest, it's very frustrating and confusing for me, but with the help and love I get from all of you, I still find joy in each new day."

Kate reached over and touched her grandpa's arm. "Don't worry, Grandpa. Our photo album will help you remember. You can look at all your old pictures, and I'm going to take some new ones so you can remember me and everyone else in the family. I'll write our names under the pictures, and I'll write your stories in the album. That way when you forget something, you'll know just where to look. It will help you. I know it will!"

Kate's grandpa took her hand in his and held it tight. "You know, Kate, I might not remember what I just did and I may seem a little more confused than I used to be, but — no matter what — the important memories of my life will forever be in my heart. I'll always remember falling in love with your grandma. She's still the most beautiful woman in the world. I'll always remember how I felt when your mom got married and how you looked the day you were born. I'll always remember how proud I was to serve my country and how much I love my family." ❧ Kate sat back as Grandpa talked about his life. He told her how proud he was of her mother and his sons . . . how much he enjoyed his grandkids . . . how grateful he was to God for giving him the greatest life a man could ask for. "No doubt about it," he said, "I'm the luckiest man on Earth."

As Grandpa talked on, Kate looked down at her pictures — pictures of Grandpa getting married . . . pictures of him on his honeymoon . . . pictures of him with his kids when they were little. ☺ Kate rocked back in her chair and stared out at the beautiful day. More than ever, she understood how lucky she was to have her grandpa. Kate had no idea what tomorrow would bring, but she knew that what was happening right then and there, at that moment, between her and Grandpa, was love . . . pure and simple. She could feel it. It felt good. It felt warm. It felt peaceful. Kate knew she'd remember that special feeling . . . forever and ever.

Resources

Resources for Families Affected by Alzheimer's Disease

Alzheimer's Association
www.alz.org   (800) 272-3900
- *A comprehensive site with information dedicated to research, causes, caregivers, and links to doctors*
- *Provides information to find local chapters*
- *Contact center is available 24 hours*

Safe Return Hotline
www.alz.org/ResourceCenter/Programs/
SafeReturn.htm   (888) 572-8566
- *Provides information on how to join the Alzheimer's Association's identification-registry program as a precaution for patients who may wander away from home*

Alzheimer's Disease Education and Referral Center
www.alzheimers.org   (800) 438-4380
- *Service of the National Institute on Aging*
- *Links to 29 Alzheimer's Disease Centers across the U.S.*

Resources

A.W.A.R.E.: Alzheimer's Women's Association
  for Resources and Education
  www.alzdallas.org   (800) 515-8201
  • *Provides support and assistance to persons affected by
     Alzheimer's disease and related disorders, as well as
     to their families and other caregivers*
  • *Encourages and supports research into the cause,
     improved diagnosis, prevention, and cure of
     Alzheimer's disease*

Alzheimer's Disease Cooperative Study
  http://adcs.ucsd.edu   (858) 622-5880
  • *Web site is part of a larger Web community that offers
     information about Alzheimer's disease research, treatment,
     and related topics*
  • *More than 25 affiliate schools and universities involved
     in the study of Alzheimer's can be linked through the
     ADCS Web site at http://adcs.ucsd.edu*

Resources

National Institute on Aging
www.nia.nih.gov   (301) 496-1752
- *Provides leadership in aging research, training, health information dissemination, and other programs relevant to aging and older people*
- *NIA is the primary federal agency on Alzheimer's disease research*

Alzheimer's Disease International
www.Alz.co.uk   011 44 207 620 3011
- *London-based organization with members from 66 countries worldwide*
- *Encourages research and the formation of new Alzheimer's associations*
- *Looks to stimulate public and political awareness on a national and international level, and to support and strengthen member associations in their activities*